Kaya Keeps Her Cool

Copyright: © 2005 Baumhaus Verlag, Frankfurt am Main, Germany
Original title: KAYA, FREI UND STARK – KAYA BLEIBT COOL
Cover and inside illustrations: Baumhaus Verlag
Printed in Germany, 2008
Translated by Karen Nickel Anhalt
Typeset by Roberta L. Melzl
Editor: Bobbie Chase

ISBN: 1-933343-75-3

Stabenfeldt, Inc.
457 North Main Street
Danbury, CT 06811
www.pony.us

Gaby Hauptmann

Kaya Keeps Her Cool

Translated by Karen Nickel Anhalt

For Caroline, our lively girl

*"Love horses and look after them; for they deserve
your tenderness; treat them as you do your children;
nourish them as you do friends of the family,
and blanket them with care.
For the love of God, do not be negligent
for you will regret it in this life and the next."*

Sidi-Aomar, Companion of the Prophet Mohammed

Rehearsal was indescribably frantic again and everything seemed to go utterly wrong. The adult quadrille was a mess! No one could imagine that they would ever be ready in time for the Christmas pageant.

Kaya and the others had already saddled up their ponies for the jumping quadrille, but left them in their stalls while they stood around outside the riding hall, waiting and shivering in the cold.

"How much longer is that supposed to go on?" asked Mia impatiently, as she brushed a dark brown curl from her face. She was thirteen years old, and although she was quite slim she looked like a prize boxer just now, with her feet planted in a wide stance and her arms crossed in front of her chest.

Kaya stood on top of an upside-down pail and peered over the swinging door into the arena. "They keep messing up their moves," she said to the girls behind her. "That's what their problem is. And they keep yelling at each other."

"Grownups," harrumphed Reni. "What else can you expect!"

Freddy shivered. "I'm about to turn into an icicle! Let's go wait in the clubroom instead."

It was already quite crowded in there, and several people had brought their dogs along to dry their wet fur near the heater, which was already piled high with damp horse blankets. A few pairs of riding boots stood against the wall. The stench of wet people and animals assaulted Kaya as she opened the door. "Yuk!" she said and held her nose – although that didn't help much. Her friends shoved her into the room.

Claudia staged a Christmas riding pageant in her small stable every other year. The show always included a colorful mix of entertainment involving youths, adults and children, and at the end of the show Santa Claus never failed to show up. The program always revolved around some sort of moving story about a horse or a person and there was always a special highlight… and the rehearsals were always so chaotic that no one believed they'd be ready in time for the show.

Today was the dress rehearsal, and things were especially bad. The 16 riders in the arena simply couldn't coordinate with each other. First they didn't come together with their horses, then they forgot the next formation – it was a hopeless mess. And while everyone was of good cheer in the clubroom, in the arena, the mood was getting increasingly testy. Finally Claudia cut it short. She had never done anything like that before!

The girls looked at each other with expressions of shock. Were they supposed to lead their ponies into the hall now? Or was that the end or the entire rehearsal for the day? Or maybe even of the whole pageant? The clubroom had gone silent. Even the adults looked confused as they watched one rider after the other leave the hall.

"Now what?" asked Mia, breaking the silence.

Her innocent question gave everyone else the signal to start talking again. Suddenly everyone was jabbering and a few people even went outside. The dogs barked and the chaos was complete when one of the horses in the hall bolted from his rider and bucked across the arena. Claudia stood in the middle, her arms hanging limply at her sides. Even from a distance and through the dirty window of the clubroom, it was pretty obvious that she would have liked nothing better than to be beamed out of there that very second.

"Okay, let's get going," said Kaya.

"To do what?" asked Cindy, the freckle-faced redhead, as she scratched her nose.

"To ask what's next!" said Kaya and shrugged her shoulders. She couldn't believe that Claudia would call the whole thing off. After all, her Christmas pageants were too well known because they were so entertaining – and free.

The fact that there was no entrance fee no doubt helped make them so eagerly anticipated. Where else could you get something for nothing? Claudia managed to pull it off. The audience sat on bales of hay that were stacked at the short end of the hall to make a sort of grandstand. They came for the fun of drinking mulled cider, eating hot dogs and enjoying the festive mood, the entertainment and later, of course, the gossip. Claudia's Christmas party was quite an event in this small community, a fact that sixteen clueless adults couldn't change.

Kaya went out and bumped into Tracy, who was waiting at the entrance with her Andalusian stallion, Brioso.

"What's going on here?" asked Tracy, and Brioso threw his black head up, tossing his lush mane.

"Panic on the Titanic," smirked Kaya. When Tracy gave her a strange look, Kaya added, "Claudia just broke off the adult quadrille. I was just on my way to ask her what we should do now."

"That's pretty courageous for a dress rehearsal," said Tracy, and she grinned back. With her height, her long dark hair and her reed thin figure, she and her Andalusian fit together extremely well. She kept Brioso in his own stable and only joined the others here for special events or to teach courses on groundwork.

"Will you let me know what happens?"

Kaya nodded and pushed her way through the agitated crowd of people and animals to the entrance of the hall. Claudia was still standing alone in the middle of the arena. Obviously no one dared to go over to her. Had she really flipped out? Although she was capable of getting testy with people, for the most part Claudia was a gentle soul who tried to please everyone.

Kaya opened the gate just wide enough to slip through. Like most of her friends, she was 13 years old and quite flexible and muscular from all her athletics.

"Do you mind if I bother you?"

Claudia turned around toward her. Her face was marked by the tension of the situation, but seeing Kaya, who usually barged right in instead of carefully tiptoeing around, made her burst out laughing.

"I'm not going to bite!" she said, "At least not right away!"

"Thank goodness!" answered Kaya, and she laughed, too.

Claudia took a deep breath.

"To answer your question, we'll continue in a few minutes. And we'll cut back to eight riders, that's all."

"That's it?" Now Kaya was a little disappointed. No scandal, no rioting, nothing at all, just a normal

dress rehearsal. Even though it looked quite different a
minute ago.

"All right then, we'll wait a little longer," she said
and turned around to go.

"That would make me happy," said Claudia. It was
hard to tell whether she was joking or not.

Kaya informed Tracy right away and then slipped
into the clubroom. This could take a while.

Poor Flying Dream, Kaya's horse, was saddled up
and snaffled, but all he could do now was stand around
and wait.

Her friends and most of the other people had
already left the clubroom. It was nearly empty and the
atmosphere was less than pleasant. Empty bottles were
everywhere, half empty glasses stood on the tables
and opened packages of chips and snacks were strewn
about. Kaya, who sometimes helped out in her parents'
restaurant, couldn't bear to see such a mess, so she started
to clear away some of the garbage and dirty glasses.

The radio played Christmas music in the
background. Kaya watched the first rider get back
into the ring and was only listening with half an ear
when the music was interrupted for an important
announcement. At first she didn't really comprehend
what was being reported, but then it hit her – the radio

announcer was talking about horses that ran away from somewhere and were loose on a country road.

Good heavens, she thought. It had snowed quite a bit in the past few days, which meant that it was slippery as ice on the roads tonight. It would be next to impossible for a driver to see the horses in the dark. And no driver could brake fast enough to avoid hitting a horse that suddenly appeared from out of nowhere. Kaya was annoyed with herself for not hearing where it was that the horses had been spotted.

She tried to think what the quickest way to find out the location of the horses would be. Should she just wait until the next announcement? At least none of the horses from this stable were missing; someone would have noticed.

She was still thinking about what to do when she saw Claudia through the window, reaching into her pocket for her cell phone. She must have forgotten to turn it off. That was something she almost never forgot to do – this really was an unusual evening! Claudia looked at the display, then at the riders – they were just getting back into position – and then she answered the phone. It only took a moment and then she suddenly looked agitated and Kaya saw her frantically waving the other riders over.

Now what was going on?

But Claudia wasn't just waving the other riders over; she was also waving to Kaya. No doubt about that. But what could she possibly want from her? Had someone forgotten the bandages? Or were there horse pies in the arena that needed to be cleared? Kaya waved back and tried not to show her reluctance. It was really cold out there and she didn't feel like leaving the warmth of the clubroom to walk into the ice-cold riding hall. Besides, with all the interruptions, it had gotten later and later and she was annoyed because she had rented "Pirates of the Caribbean: The Curse of the Black Pearl" and was looking forward to watching Johnny Depp. Right now she felt like she was the one who was cursed.

Dreamy was probably starting to think she was nuts. He was not the kind of pony who enjoyed standing around doing nothing. He'd probably fall asleep before they even started their jumping quadrille and then sleepwalk over the obstacles. And where had the rest of her friends, the "Wild Amazons," gone? Were they hanging out among the hay bales, eating chips and drinking sodas? The little hideaway they had built up over the years sure was a lot more appealing than Claudia's wave to her.

Oh well.

"Coming through," she called before she walked into the arena. Announcing that was an absolute must to avoid crashing into someone else or being knocked over by a horse. Claudia immediately approached her. The riders were huddled in a group debating something – this situation was starting to look better!

Kaya stood still.

"I just got a call from the police," said Claudia, out of breath. "Five horses broke out of who knows where and are making one of the back roads unsafe. We have to capture them!"

"We?" Kaya looked around involuntarily. "What do you mean, 'we'?"

"Since nobody has contacted the authorities, no one seems to miss them – and no one knows where they come from."

Hey! This could be an opportunity! Maybe, if they were valuable jumping horses Kaya could just keep one of them. Or maybe they circus horses, like from Ringling Brothers? Or maybe a European Championship pony, like the one her friend Chris's parents recently bought for him, a hundred thousand dollar sensation?

"Where are they?" asked Kaya. Her feelings of listlessness evaporated.

"Somewhere between here and the river!"

That road went through the woods and was so full of curves that it had extremely poor visibility.

"Oh my gosh! And how are we supposed to catch them?"

"The police will secure the road first. Then we'll take the horse transporters, gather up all the adults here and head out!"

"And what about our dress rehearsal?"

"We'll do it during our main event!"

Oh no. This could be a real mess. Kaya followed Claudia and in no time they had rounded up all the adults and kids. They quickly took the saddles and snaffles off their ponies, put them back in their stalls and got into the cars out in the parking lot.

Kaya was just about to get in with Claudia when she saw Chris and his mother turn the corner. She could recognize their jeep anywhere; it was absolutely unmistakable, especially since most of the time, Chris was sitting in it. Chris, her secret crush, the 15-year-old who looked more like a surfer boy than a show jumper. "I'll be right there," she called to Claudia and slammed the door closed. She walked toward Simone Walden, Chris's mom, waving both her arms. Simone stopped her jeep right away and waited while Chris lowered his window and leaned out.

"Where's the fire?" He pointed to all the cars

pulling out of the parking lot at the same time. The big horse truck pulled into the lot, with Claudia's husband at the wheel.

"Well, it's something like that," said Kaya quickly. "Five horses escaped and are walking on the road between here and the river. The police called and asked us to help capture them."

"Do you have a lasso with you?" Chris furrowed his brow and Kaya thought he looked cute.

"Do you want to ride with us? Then we can help out, too!" said Mrs. Walden. Finally, her salvation! This woman was so cool!

"Oh, yes!" Kaya got in back and sent a text message to her sister. She would take care of letting their parents know that she'd be coming home a little bit later than planned tonight.

"Five horses? How can you not notice when five horses are missing?" mused Simone Walden. She was wearing a fluffy down jacket and a knit cap on her head. She always looked more like she could be Chris's older sister than his mother, and usually wore jeans and T-shirts, even though she was a successful tax attorney. Her husband, on the other hand, was always elegantly dressed, looking every bit the businessman from head to toe, even when he was on vacation.

A few weeks earlier Kaya had accompanied the Waldens to a training center where they had examined and bought Wild Thing, an outstanding jumper pony. She had been allowed to test it in dressage and was going to ride it in the Christmas pageant as part of the youth quadrille, one of the highlights of the evening. But now it looked like the highlight of her evening would end up being on a dark country road.

They could see a red police light flashing in the woods ahead of them and Simone cut her speed. "Aha, the police are already here," she said; "that's good news." She pointed to the glove compartment. "Take a look to see if our flashlight is in there. It should be... unless you forgot to put it back again."

"Me? Why do I always get blamed?!" Chris threw her an outraged look before opening the glove compartment. He pulled out a black flashlight and turned it on right away. "So there! And it works, too!"

"Your luck!" His mother smiled and slowed down as they reached the area the police had secured.

Their car rolled up to a policeman who stood on the shoulder and Simone rolled down her window. "Are you part of the search party?" he asked.

"Yes, we hope we'll be able to catch them," she answered. He nodded and allowed her to drive past.

"Kaya, could you take a look in the back – do you see a halter and lead?"

Kaya leaned over the back of her seat and confirmed that they were there.

"Great!" Simone gave her son a playful wink. "I guess there's an upside to never putting your stuff away."

"It looks like there are apples and snacks, too," added Kaya.

"Well isn't that nice?" said Chris's mother. "Are the apples still edible?"

Kaya picked up one. "Well, at least they aren't moldy."

"It's a good thing my husband almost never uses this car, or he'd have a major fit," laughed Simone and pointed ahead. "So, folks, there are the others. Let's go see what the situation is."

The woods were so dark and dense and silent that the group might as well have been deep in an Amazonian jungle. The freezing cold didn't fit the picture, though. But the way they were walking next to each other through the woods, each carrying a more or less powerful flashlight, sure looked pretty spooky.

Kaya walked side by side with Chris and that alone made the adventure worth it. Regardless of what happened with the horses, and even after their little expedition was over and she was back in the stable filling hay nets, nothing could change the fact that she'd gotten to have this little *tête a tête* with Chris, even if she couldn't do a *pas de deux* with his pony. She smiled at the thought – too bad she couldn't say it out loud. The only thing that bothered her was that there were too many people rustling through the woods. Finally she told Chris what she had been thinking. "You can't catch a horse this way." They reached the top of a hill with at least 20 other people in a row. Most were out of breath because not only was it all uphill, but the terrain was also extremely uneven and full of branches and roots.

"Does anyone really know that the horses walked in this direction?" said a loud voice from somewhere in the middle of their group. It was Klaus Sonnig, Mia's father. He was right. Why were they walking here, of all places? The horses could just as easily be on the other side.

"A motorist saw them walk up here and reported it to the police." This time it was a woman's voice.

"That was probably hours ago, and we seem to be mistaking the horses for snails. They've got to be somewhere totally different now." The flashlights swung around and everyone walked closer together. They looked like mountain men, their faces obscured by their scarves and hats and their breath frozen white.

Most of them carried ropes or halters in their hands or wrapped around their waists. A few of them stomped their feet because the cold was creeping in through the thin leather soles of their riding boots.

"Now what?" they asked Claudia who was standing in the middle of the group. She had a red scarf wrapped around her head.

She sighed and was searching for the right answer when her cell phone rang. It was her husband Rick. "Come this way and hurry – they're here!" he spoke so loudly that almost everyone standing near her could hear it through the tiny loudspeaker in her phone. In fact, they probably would have heard him with or without the phone because Claudia's husband has a very powerful voice. They turned on their heels and ran down the hill. Some slid and held onto trees and a few tripped and fell. When they all made it to the bottom, they saw that the ruckus had frightened off the horses. Of course. Rick stood in the light from his truck's headlights and just shook his head.

"Like a herd of camels," he said and motioned toward the pack. "I think it would be best if at least half of our group goes home and no more than ten people stay here. Anything else just doesn't make sense."

The way he said that – Claudia must have been

proud of him. Most of the others were relieved to be off the hook. "It really is freezing cold!" said the heavy husband of one of the riders, huffing and puffing as he dug his car keys out of his pocket. Simone Walden nodded to him sympathetically. "Women are better at tolerating the cold," she said. "They have a different layer of fat."

"That must be true," he said and plopped down into his car.

Kaya looked around. In addition to herself, all her girlfriends had also remained. Then there was Mrs. Walden, Chris, Claudia and Rick. Five girls, two women, one boy and one man. That was more than enough.

"Which way did they go?" Simone asked, growling in a completely unladylike manner because the snow had suddenly started coming down heavily. The snowflakes looked like huge clumps dancing in the bright headlights. In a flash, the road was covered in a white carpet of snow. Simone pulled the collar of her down jacket tighter around her neck and stuck her hands deep in the pockets.

"It's not so bad," said Kaya, who didn't feel very cold despite the fact that her quilted riding jacket had gotten too small for her since last year. She brushed the snow out of her hair and laughed.

"Not so bad?" repeated Claudia.

"Yes, because now we can see their tracks!"

"A girl scout – I knew it all along!" Simone nodded to her approvingly. Even better, Chris gave her a pat on the back. "Off you go, you Apache!" he said and gave her a cheeky grin.

Kaya turned around. Behind them the red police light was still spinning and blinking. The policemen themselves had probably sought the warmth of their cars long ago, trusting in the horse people or at least hoping that the horses would instinctively find their way back to their stable. From where they were standing, they couldn't see the roadblock at the other end of the road because of all the curves and the dense forest.

"Let's just walk along the side of the road," suggested Kaya. "If they're anywhere near here, we'll see their tracks. And Rick can drive slowly behind us in his truck so that we can load them right in when we catch them."

Claudia nodded. "Good idea! Do you have ropes and some sort of bait to attract them? We'd better not make any hasty moves when we see them. We need to stay as still as possible and lure them to us."

Kaya gave Chris a meaningful look. The time his own pony broke away, he did everything wrong. But that was several weeks ago. He had probably forgotten the whole thing already.

They walked in the light of the headlights. The truck behind them made the strangest noises, growling and groaning. That old bucket of bolts had seen better days, but at the stable they were ecstatic that they even had the vehicle. Without it, they'd have to drive to horse shows in an endless line of horse trailers. For one thing, they didn't have that many drivers, and of the drivers that they had not all of them had the time to go to shows. And then there was the question of horse trailers, which you didn't exactly find at the bottom of a Cracker Jack box. Riding could be a cumbersome sport!

Kaya took a deep breath and then looked over to her friends. They had their heads close together and were whispering. Probably about her. They certainly had reason to, thought Kaya. Normally, they would concoct plans like this together, talking things over and sharing their adventures. But now, in this big adventure, they were separated by Chris, which they probably thought was unacceptable. No girl liked it if a friend started acting odd because of a boy. Hopefully they'd still talk to her afterwards. She looked over to them again and caught the eye of Mia, who winked at her. So it couldn't be all that bad, no unforgivable crime committed, or Mia would have stuck out her tongue.

"Stop!" said Claudia suddenly. They had had such a good walking rhythm that her outburst seemed like a disturbance. But the whole pack of them stopped and saw why Claudia had given the command. On the road in front of them, they could see black tracks on the white snow. Deer, elk, wild boar, people – or could it be horses? Claudia and Simone took a few steps closer, the truck stopped and the girls and Chris waited. Claudia turned around and nodded. She beamed and looked a little like a treasure hunter closing in on the loot. The red scarf on her head was almost completely white and her cheeks glowed, although Kaya couldn't tell if that was from the cold or the excitement. At any rate, she looked more like an Eskimo than like Claudia Hartzler.

She raised her hand, which seemed to signal "Quiet!" Then, despite the grumbling of the truck's engine, they could hear the patter of hooves.

The horses! Claudia gave Rick a signal to turn off the motor, and it went silent with a sigh. First it was totally quiet. And then! There it was again. This time they could hear it more clearly: quiet horse steps. They stood there, as if frozen to the spot. It was so delightfully creepy there on a road in the middle of the woods during a snowstorm on a moonless night with the only light coming from the headlights of a truck... and now something that none of them could see was getting closer.

Kaya couldn't stand horror movies, and at that moment she knew why. Unforeseeable events were just not her bag. She liked to have a clear view of things well in advance and wanted to know what was coming at her from around the corner, whether she was on snow shoveling duty, or whether she had to write a report for school. She couldn't stand alarm clocks that didn't stick to any particular schedule.

But right now an alarm clock kind of a situation was about to happen. She nearly grabbed Chris's arm. He looked calm standing there next to her, but she didn't buy the cool act. All of them were totally tense, even Simone Walden, who always looked like she had everything under control, including her husband.

They stood there, completely motionless. Suddenly, a large black shadow came around the bend and stopped in front of them, rooted to the spot. The only thing they could think of doing was to start babbling at it. "Hoho," and "Come here, fella." But the fella didn't want to come here and he turned right around and disappeared again. All of them looked at each other, dumbfounded, and then slowly began walking again. This time Kaya walked ahead with her friends. The girls usually had a calming effect on horses. They weren't that big and their voices were soft and friendly. Kaya firmly believed that horses had a certain instinct for what was good for them and what wasn't.

Now all the girls had to do was prove to the horses that they were good for them.

Kaya, Mia, Cindy, Reni and Freddy walked in a row ahead of the others around the curve in the road. They stopped and saw a wall of horses. It looked very threatening in the darkness, since the truck's headlights barely reached this far. And while the horse's legs on the white snow were easy enough to make out, the rest of their dark bodies blended into the dark background.

The girls stood still and Kaya suddenly found herself thinking about the Middle Ages, despite the fact that she'd gotten a bad grade on the last report she wrote about that era for her history class. She figured that back then, the armies of enemy kings used to stand across from each other just like this. Startled by the unexpected encounter, each side hesitated uncertainly, waiting for the opposing side to react. Who'd make the first move? And would it be friendly or hostile?

Kaya wasn't planning to march blindly over to the

strange horses. Instead, she resorted to a trick. She had
carrots in her left pocket and a plastic bag full of pellets
in her right pocket. She had taken them out of the
trough for Dreamy. She liked to reward him whenever
he had to do something outside of his normal routine,
like the jumping quadrille rehearsal at the unusual
evening hour.

She rustled the plastic bag. Heaven only knows why
plastic bags are so highly regarded in the all-natural
horse world, but immediately the first four legs started
to fidget impatiently. It was like a shadow play. She
couldn't see anything on top, but on the bottom, she
could see movement. Kaya rustled the bag again and
took a step forwards. She could feel everyone's eyes
fixed on her. If she made a false move now, then she'd
be the scapegoat of the evening.

Trust in yourself and then others will trust in you too,
she said to herself. It was a phrase her mother often said
to her. And although she had no idea why she suddenly
found herself thinking about that, she made up her
mind to trust in herself. So she took another big step
forward and rustled the plastic bag some more as she
took out the food.

One of the shadows separated from the group
in front of her, first slowly, then more quickly, and

approached her. It strode forcefully over to her. And it wasn't some small animal like a foal or something... no, it was a pony. It got closer and boldly nudged her bag. Kaya gave him a handful and suddenly there was Mia next to her, shoving a carrot into his mouth and grabbing him by his halter. Mia was just fantastic, Kaya thought.

She took another step forward, but it was as if that pony had set an avalanche into motion. Suddenly all of them came over, surrounded her and gently tried to tear the plastic bag out of her hand. Now all of the others had stepped in to help. Armed with carrots, snacks, leads and halters, in a flash they had four horses and one pony roped up.

But they didn't feel like they were out of the woods yet, so to speak. If one of the horses were to panic, then they'd have a real problem, especially because of the snow. With reassuring phrases and a constant stream of snacks, they managed to lead the animals around the bend and lure them over to the truck. But then they stopped, rooted to the spot. That wasn't a surprise, really. These weren't tournament horses, so this container on wheels must have looked like a monster to them.

Claudia signaled to Rick and he stayed up front in

the cab. He waited, watching in his rearview mirror until he saw them disappear behind the next curve in the road, before he started up his diesel motor and turned the truck around.

They made their way back to the stable with a police escort. Kaya took over the pony that had first approached her and sent Mia up ahead to the police car. The policemen were to turn off their flashing lights and then drive slowly ahead of the crowd with only their headlights flashing. They proceeded, and after a half hour's hike, they all reached the stable, safe and sound.

In the meantime, five stalls had been cleared and prepared. The ponies that were usually in them had been moved in with other ponies with whom they were familiar and friendly. Chris's star pony, Wild Thing, which had only been there for the dress rehearsal, had been moved back to her home stable, vacating her guest stall for the others.

They marched into the stable in silence. Most of the riders were still there, and in the meantime a few parents had joined them. Only after the horses were put safely into their stalls – and were devouring their food as if they were starving to death after spending weeks on the road – only then did things get noisy.

"How can this be?" asked Kaya. She was standing

next to Chris as she watched the pony at the trough. He had sunk his head so deeply into the trough that they could hardly see him.

"In a minute he'll climb all the way in," commented Chris and Kaya had to laugh, although actually it was a pitiful sight. The little fellow was just skin and bones. His hooves were overgrown, his coat was shaggy, and he was probably riddled with parasites.

"It reminds me a little of the manger at Christmas," said Kaya, as she cupped her hands together and puffed into them. Her fingers had gotten desperately cold during their long hike back.

"It makes me think of a small circus that doesn't have the funds to make it through the winter!"

"Come on, quit joking!" She didn't even want to think about that. "If that were the case, then there must be llamas and elephants wandering around out there, too."

"And clowns," added Chris, but Kaya absolutely couldn't laugh about that.

She was silent for a while, and before long her four girlfriends came over to her. "The four horses look like this, too," said Reni and shook her head. "Either they've been wandering around lost for who knows how long or their owner was a monster."

"Or he was broke."

Simone joined them and clapped her hands together. "Okay, dear girls, we've got tea, hot cider and gingerbread. Claudia's treat."

"Where?" asked Kaya suspiciously. In her head she pictured the chaotic mess in the club room.

"In the club room," said Simone and laughed when she saw Kaya's expression. "Heidi, our cleaning lady, already straightened everything up."

"What would we do without her," sighed Kaya and looked at the pony one last time. As it raised its head and quietly returned her gaze, she totally fell for him.

At seven a.m. the next morning, Kaya was already in her kitchen. Her mother, Karin, couldn't believe her eyes, considering Kaya was normally a late sleeper.

"Are you in love or something?" She laughed and tied the sash of her robe.

"You don't have to get up just because I'm up," answered Kaya. "I can manage on my own, you know."

"I know that," said her mother. "In fact, ever since Simone Walden told me that you can cook for entire families, I've known that I don't have to worry at all about you!"

Okay, that was a few weeks ago, when she stayed with the Waldens in that unbelievably idyllic cabin and played the cool chick for Chris. Now she was a few weeks older and had an even better handle on everything.

"Really, mom, why don't you just go back to bed?"

But then she sat down with her mother at the kitchen table and, while she sipped her cocoa and her mother drank her coffee, she told her every last detail.

"And we were here serving a wedding party yesterday," said her mother, annoyed. "Sometimes I have the feeling that life is passing me by. Sometime soon you'll be grown up, have kids of your own and I'll have missed out on everything."

"Oh I'm sure you'd notice something!" said Kaya, laughing. "Grandkids are guaranteed to be hard to overlook!"

Her mother laid her hand on top of Kaya's. "And why are you going to the stable so early this morning?"

Kaya took a deep breath.

"Yesterday, when all the horses were standing in front of us in the dark and we had no idea how they were going to react, and they were probably scared to death of us – well, one of them approached us. It was brave and bold and of all the people standing there trying to lure them over, it chose me. And later it looked at me in such a way that seemed to mean something more."

"What do you mean by that?"

Kaya took another sip from her cup and then wiped the cocoa mustache with the back of her hand.

"You know, he's an old soul," she said. "I think there's a certain spiritual kinship there. Right then when he looked at me, I just knew it!"

Karin Birk didn't say anything at first. She carefully contemplated what her daughter said.

"If you can wait five minutes, I'll get dressed and come with you!"

What?? This was incredible. Her mother was afraid of horses and never had any time. The tournaments Kaya went to were always on the weekends – the busiest time in the restaurant. Same thing in the evenings or when she had lessons. Her parents just couldn't share in her passion. That's something her older sister Alexa had already learned. She had spent an entire year training in a renowned stable, riding the best horses, and had been quite successful. Their parents missed out on practically all of that.

That's just the way it was.

Kaya had gotten used to it long ago. But she was overjoyed now at her mother's unexpected interest.

Twenty minutes later, they were at the stable. They met up with Rick, who was just feeding the horses.

"They look just pitiful," he said and shook his head. "And nobody misses them. They literally fell from heaven!"

"That can't be," said Karin Birk, and she looked at her daughter. "Show me the pony!"

It stood in a stall with a paddock, where an old pear tree was growing. The bark was mostly chewed off and the tree was bare because it was winter. Still, it looked idyllic. The snow that had fallen overnight had already melted and the temperatures had climbed above freezing. As they approached the paddock, the pony raised his head and looked out at Kaya through the open door. Then he snorted.

"I've got goose bumps," said Kaya's mother and Kaya automatically reached for her mother's hand, the way she did when she was a little kid. They stood there and the pony walked out to them. Kaya reached to him with the carrot she had brought for him and he took a hearty bite. Her mother didn't move at all.

"My goodness, he's skinny," she said.

"But look what a cutie he is!" replied Kaya. And really, when you stepped back and ignored how skinny he was and how shaggy his coat looked, you could see that he was a little chestnut. His legs all had the same white markings, as if he were wearing boots of the same height, and he had a large blaze that ran evenly down his head from his forehead over the bridge of his nose down to his nostrils.

"You're right," said Karin Birk and nodded. "He is something special!"

Kaya smiled like a proud mother.

"What will happen to him now?" Karin wanted to know.

"First he'll be cared for!"

"And then?"

"When his owner comes forward, then we'll look into whether this is a case for the animal welfare authorities."

"And then?"

"And then, Mom?" she gave her mother a coquettish look. "Then we'll see!"

"And what are you going to call him in the meantime?"

The answer shot right out of her.

"Whitefoot!"

"Whitefoot?" Her mother considered the name. "He's a boy, isn't he? Then why don't you call him Mr. Whitefoot?"

"Mr. Whitefoot? That sounds ridiculous."

"Then call him Sir Whitefoot!"

"Sir Whitefoot?" Kaya said the name to herself and then nodded. "That sounds elegant! That's it! Sir Whitefoot!"

By around 10 a.m. the small stable was packed to the rafters with people. Despite the fact that it was Sunday morning, all the people whom you normally only saw at important official occasions were there: Mr. Kenner, the mayor; Mr. Grover, from the local newspaper; and a few of the policemen from last night. In addition, there were plenty of horse owners and riders... news of all the action last night had spread like wildfire. They were all sitting with Claudia in the clubroom because no office had enough space for all these people. They drank coffee and debated what should be done next. Kaya snuck in to the meeting with her friends. After all, they were among the rescuers and, in Kaya's opinion, had a right to be there.

One of the policemen observed that it was strange that no one had reported the horses missing yet.

"Is it theoretically possible to overlook the fact that so many horses are missing?" he asked Claudia.

"I suppose it depends on the conditions in the stable," she answered. "In an open stable arrangement, with too many horses crowded in?" She thought for a minute, then energetically shook her head with her short brown hair. "Then all of them would have broken out and not just five. The fact that all of them are undernourished – and pretty run down, too, if you look closely – contradicts that."

The mayor grimaced and looked over to Mr. Grover who was taking down every word. "A welfare case. Is there such a thing as an equine welfare case?"

Claudia had to laugh. "A hardship case, sure, but so far we haven't had to file a single horse welfare application."

Everyone laughed with her.

Kaya frowned and gave Mia a look. What were they talking about? It was always like this: it took grownups forever to get to the point, and by the time they finally did you had fallen asleep out of boredom.

"If no one has reported them missing, then we have to conclude that someone abandoned them!"

"Abandoned?" echoed Kaya. Everyone looked at her.

"How could someone just abandon horses?" she asked. "They're so expensive!"

The mayor looked at her and shrugged his shoulders. "People abandon expensive dogs with top pedigrees. Or purebred cats. People who want to get rid of an animal and the responsibility that comes with having one don't consider that at all."

"Then we're in luck," said Freddy quietly, and she scratched her nose. Everyone heard her and laughed loudly.

"What that girl said isn't so crazy." The journalist tapped his pencil on his notebook. "After all, there are baby drop boxes…"

The laughter died down and everyone thought about what he had said. He was right. Even babies are abandoned.

"Okay, then let's get back to our problem."

The mayor looked at Claudia. "You won't be able to shelter and feed five horses for very long. So what can we do?"

The journalist answered for Claudia. "My article will run in tomorrow's edition and I'll make sure that the newswires carry the story, too. If the agencies don't want to run it, then I'll give the article to all the newspapers in the area – those animals couldn't have walked more than 75 miles. And if after that no one comes forward to report that the horses belong to them, then we'll have to start out by supporting Claudia financially so that she isn't forced to bear the entire burden alone. Then we'll look for potential buyers so we recoup the costs."

The mayor nodded. "I think that's a good idea. It makes a lot of sense."

And the policeman added, "We'll put out a bulletin to all the stations in the area. Sometimes our colleagues know of cases like this, but unless a crime is committed, they're powerless to act."

"Crime?" asked Reni.

"A complaint. Someone has to file a complaint against the owner for mistreating his horses. Or the animal protection agency has to take action. We can't go marching in just because we feel like it. We need probable cause."

"Probable cause?" repeated Freddy.

Everyone stood up because the mayor stood up. "Good," he said, "ladies and gentlemen and the members of the association of 'Wild Amazons'," he winked at the girls, "we will wait for a response and then take action."

"I can't believe he remembered our group name," whispered Cindy once he and his entourage left the room.

"That says something for him," said Kaya. She and her friends had kidnapped Flying Dream, who had been a riding school pony at the time, to prevent him from being sold. They gave themselves that moniker for a newspaper story about it. Their caper had the effect they wanted – they got a lot of publicity and Dreamy got a wonderful new owner, Chris's father. Mr. Walden bought Dreamy for his ten-year-old daughter Charlotte, and Dreamy was allowed to stay in his old stall at the stable so that Kaya could continue to train him.

"Maybe he thinks that if he remembers something like that, then later on we'll vote for him," suggested Mia.

"Not a bad strategy," said Mrs. Walden, who had just entered the clubroom. "Did I miss anything?" Kaya gave her the short version of what had happened and then they went over to Sir Whitefoot together.

The pony looked up as soon as it heard Kaya's voice and snorted quietly.

"Oh my!" said Mrs. Walden. "He's a fast learner!"

Kaya smiled. "Yes, he seems to like me somehow." They stayed at the door to his stall, stroking him and feeding him a few snacks.

"I wonder if he's even rideable," said Simone Walden and looked him over from his head to his hooves.

"Why wouldn't he be?" asked Mia, who had come along.

"Well, he has hardly any muscle tone. He doesn't look like he's been in training."

"You're right," Kaya nodded. "But don't we lose our muscle tone if we stop exercising?" Simone nodded and searched for more snacks in the pocket of her down jacket. The pony nodded his head.

"At any rate we can't just try it out. He doesn't belong to us," said Kaya.

"Yes, and first he needs to eat normally again," said Simone Walden. "The veterinarian and the farrier are coming this afternoon – that's our contribution to this situation – then we'll see what we need to do next."

"That is so wonderful of you," said Mia, amazed. Once her father found out about that, he'd surely decide to donate something too, like maybe extra food.

Kaya also thought it was cool. The Waldens were pretty groovy people. How great was it that she was in love with Chris and not someone with totally idiotic parents. You were either lucky in that respect or you weren't.

Claudia tried one more time to get people to come for a spontaneous dress rehearsal for the Christmas pageant, but it didn't work. A lot of people couldn't come because it hadn't been planned in advance, so she just allowed the normal riding activities to continue and grinned crookedly. "I'm sure God will show us a little understanding next week," she said and took a deep breath.

Kaya and her friends had holed themselves up in their Amazon nest in the hay. They had a little collection of snacks hidden in a small container where the mice couldn't get at it with drinks, chips, pretzels and chocolate.

"How can we find out where the horses came from?" asked Cindy as she chewed on her red curls.

"The article will be published tomorrow and then we'll know more," Reni was the strongest of their group. She played soccer on the side and was feared in the league as a striker. She ripped open a bag of chips and stuffed a handful in her mouth. "Anybody want some?" she mumbled as she crunched and offered the bag to her friends. The first to answer gave a demanding meow, and the girls laughed. Georgie, the stable tomcat, had crept in on them. "This isn't a mouse, Georgie; I don't think it's your taste," said Reni and held a chip in front of him. He sniffed curiously at it, and then turned away. Reni stuffed the chip into her own mouth and grinned mischievously at Mia, who had raised her eyebrows. "Our bodies need a few bacteria – otherwise our immune systems won't develop and we'll be sick all the time!"

"Well, you certainly won't have any problems, then," said Freddy dryly as she dug another chip out of the bag in Reni's hand. "Come on, pass the bag. I want another one!"

Cindy stuck the strand of hair that she had been chewing behind her ear, gave Freddy a cheeky wink and asked smugly, "Could it be that I saw you at the schoolyard last Friday with Josh?" Right away all of the girls looked extremely interested and drew in closer.

"Oh, Josh!" purred Mia. "Isn't he a fancy one!"

"That's something you only say about horses, you idiots!" Freddy tugged so hard on the bottom corner of the chip bag that the package ripped and all the chips fell in the straw.

"Great, now you can have a few more antibodies," said Kaya to Reni and made a sweeping gesture.

"Did you have to pull so hard?!" Reni snapped at Freddy, but Freddy just shrugged.

"Well?" Cindy wasn't going to give up. "What's up with Josh?"

"What do you think is up?" said Freddy ungraciously. "He's good-looking, he's 17 and he has a girlfriend!"

"No!" the reaction came in unison.

"Yes!" answered Freddy.

"What a jerk," said Kaya. "Doesn't he realize what he's doing?"

"Not everyone's as lucky as you are!" Freddy gave her a look and Kaya went back to digging some of the chips out of the straw.

The others went silent and Kaya suddenly had the feeling that they were all looking at her. She looked up at them only to see them staring back at her, waiting.

"Okay people, there's not much to tell there either. He still thinks my big sister is more interesting than I am!"

"Hmm!" Cindy thought it over. "How about a magic potion?"

"Magic potion? That's ridiculous." Reni energetically scratched her head. "That's something you only get in children's books. He just needs a knock on the head to snap him out of it."

"Wait a second," said Freddy and listened closely.

"What?" Reni cocked her head.

"Somebody's calling."

"Oh yeah? Is the potion working already?" joked Kaya, but the others told her to shush.

Kaya listened closely, too. "That's Claudia," she concluded.

"Yes, and she's calling your name, Kaya!" added Reni.

All of girls looked at Kaya and she groaned. "Why is it always me?"

They all grinned and Reni shrugged her shoulders. "It must be one of those laws of nature!"

"Baloney!" Kaya got up. "I'll go see what's up!"

Claudia stood in the courtyard waiting for her.

"We just let the new ones out to run, but the little fellow keeps fooling around!" she said.

"What do you mean, 'fooling around'?" asked Kaya.

"Well, the first thing he did was scramble up into the bleachers, and we had a heck of a time getting him back down again."

"The bleachers?" Kaya looked dumbfounded. "What do you mean, the bleachers?" It was chilly and she zipped her jacket.

"The bales of hay that we stacked for the Christmas pageant."

"He climbed up *those*? That's pretty crazy."

"And after we lured him down with a few snacks, he assumed they were a reward for what he'd just done and scrambled right back up again!"

Kaya had to laugh out loud. "Oh no, what a mess!"

"Well, it wasn't really so bad," said Claudia, "but he is a totally playful fellow, a real clown. Tracy is doing some groundwork right now and she'll work with him next, if you like. It might be fun for him!"

Kaya was happy. Groundwork was all about training a horse's concentration. Some of the simpler exercises dealt with the horse responding to a few specific cues given by his trainer. When a horse is being led, he has to react to a certain cue that means he should stand still, and then another that means to continue walking. Next comes the Spanish walk, curtsey, and so on right up to lying down. At her cue, Tracy's stallions even reared up and walked on their hind legs or laid down under the rider and then stood up again. They were practically fit for performing in the circus.

Kaya had already taken a course from Tracy with Dreamy, but Dreamy was too macho. When he got the cue for "stop," he always took one step more than he was supposed to. And when he was cued to start walking again, he always waited for a count of three before obeying. When he was in the right mood he performed masterfully, but if he didn't feel like it, then there was nothing anyone could do. He was incredibly obstinate and all the tricks in the world wouldn't get him to change.

Now, if Sir Whitefoot was as big a clown as Claudia seemed to think, then things could get pretty hilarious.

Kaya put on his halter, grabbed a lead and went into the riding hall with him. Tracy was just training with Golondrina, an Andalusian mare that was the daughter of one of her stallions. She was still young, but was already quite accomplished. Kaya entered the arena with Sir Whitefoot and he found what he saw to be very interesting, indeed. Golondrina was just doing the curtsey, stretching her left front leg forward and kneeling down with the right while lowering her head. As she was getting up from her well-executed curtsey, she got a treat from Tracy, who always kept her pockets full of snacks.

"Warm him up, first," she called to Kaya. Kaya tried, but the pony resisted.

"He'd rather watch," she shouted.

"Then let him watch!" Tracy called back.

Golondrina lay down on cue and stood up again. Tracy reached into her pocket again. The mare stretched her lovely neck and looked past her trainer to Sir Whitefoot, who returned her gaze.

"Look out or they'll fall in love," joked Tracy, and patted the white horse's neck. "If you'd like, you can come over right now and I'll have someone lead Golondrina out."

Kaya was excited.

The pony eyed Tracy, then her crop, and finally her bulging jacket pocket. The pocket was reason enough for him to step closer. Tracy had to laugh and called the mare's owner. She came quickly and led Golondrina away.

"All right, let's have a look!" She loosely led the pony in a circle a few times. Then she stopped it and gently touched his front leg with her crop. He was supposed to feel that the crop wasn't something he needed to fear. Touching him with the crop was only supposed to get his attention. He lowered his head and observed what Tracy was doing. Then he lay down suddenly and raised his head in anticipation of a treat. Kaya and Tracy looked at each other.

"He must have seen Golondrina do that!" Tracy shook her head. "Something like that has never happened to me before!" She gave him his treat and he stood up and shook the peat out of his coat. He waited for the next cue.

"Hmm!" Tracy looked at him. "What are we going to do with this one?" Kaya shrugged her shoulders.

"Try something else, I guess. Maybe leading?"

He hadn't seen that yet, so it was new to him. The lead hand up meant "stop" and when it was lowered, that meant "go." Sir Whitefoot seemed fascinated by the exercise. He pricked his ears, looked interested, and by the third round he knew exactly when he should stop and when he should go again.

"This is incredible!" Tracy stood with him, stroked his neck and gave him a treat. "Do you think they escaped from the circus?"

Kaya walked over to them. "Maybe out of a winter camp. Are the others like this, too?"

"I've only seen them walking so far. But I'd say they're just regular horses. Nothing special, especially in the condition they're in."

"I know what you mean. The vet and the farrier are coming later. The Waldens are paying for it."

"Wow, that's what I call generous!" Tracy nodded. "Now we'll try something else…" She tapped the pony's front leg again with her crop. He was only supposed to respond by lifting his leg. It was a simple exercise in concentration along the lines of "where do I feel something and how do I react?"

Sir Whitefoot reacted by stretching back, with both feet together. He stretched like a cat. It was almost a curtsey, although he hadn't figured it out all the way. But that didn't stop him from immediately lifting his head to get his treat.

"This one's a real prodigy!" said Tracy, clearly impressed. "It's a good thing we don't have a piano standing around or he'd try that, too."

"I think he's sweet!" said Kaya and hugged him.

"He's more than that," said Tracy, who had studied animal psychology. "He's a very clever fellow, who knows how to win people's hearts!"

"You mean he's calculating?" asked Kaya, almost disappointed.

"No, I think that he's developed a very keen sense of survival. Who knows what he's already experienced."

"Claudia says he's about six years old."

"You see," said Tracy, "that can be long or short depending on where you grow up."

Together Kaya and Tracy led Sir Whitefoot back to his stall and observed how he quickly and assuredly went in, as if he had been doing it all his life.

"Can I tell you a secret?" said Kaya quietly.

Tracy, who was much taller, bent down to her. "Can I tell you that I already know what it is?" she whispered back. They looked at each other like co-conspirators.

"Should we research it ourselves?" Tracy continued.

"But how?" asked Kaya.

They leaned together against the lower door of Sir Whitefoot's stall. He kept an eye on them while luxuriously nibbling on his hay.

"I'm familiar with just about all of the riding stables in the area because I give lessons everywhere… " Tracy began.

"Do you mean you know… ?" interrupted Kaya breathlessly.

"No, but I think we can find out pretty quickly! They didn't come very far or we would have heard about it earlier. If think we need to search within a ten to fifteen-mile radius. Really, ten miles should be enough."

"That close?"

Tracy nodded.

They looked like two sisters standing there next to each other. The one with her extremely long legs in leather chaps, the other in her riding pants, young and slim.

"Is this a private audience?"

Chris's voice! Kaya whipped her head around.

Tracy gave him a look first and then Kaya, and her eyes sparkled with satisfaction. Chris's hair looked so wild that Tracy instantly recognized how hard he must have worked to make it look that way. She could see in Kaya's face that the guy had quite an effect on her. Animal psychology was a broad science and she couldn't help smiling.

"How's the little guy doing?" Chris asked Kaya about the horse.

Kaya bubbled over. There was already so much to tell after such a short time.

As Tracy tried to subtly withdraw, Kaya suddenly remembered what they had been talking about.

"Oh, wait a second!" she said and pulled on Tracy's arm. Excitedly, she told Chris about what Tracy had been saying.

"Should we go visit all of them?" he asked.

"First we need to come up with a coherent strategy

and then we'll get going," said Tracy. It was obvious that Chris wasn't quite sure if she was kidding or not.

"Sounds good," he said finally and nodded.

"I think it sounds like three year's worth of office work," said Kaya. "My father always says that drawing up elaborate plans never accomplishes very much. Too much theory!"

Tracy laughed heartily. "But we're not in politics here, or city planning." She crossed her arms. "I've already got a strategy, and if you've got a little time we can get right down to business!"

"All right!" Kaya was thrilled. "I'll round up the girls!" She was about to run off, but then stopped and turned to Chris. "You're coming, too, aren't you?"

"I'd like to," he said slowly and frowned, "but we're having company this afternoon – relatives, and I have to be there."

"Really?" Kaya couldn't believe it. A guy as grown-up as Chris had to be around when uncles and aunts came over? The incredulous expression on her face made him blush. Was he embarrassed now or what...? Suddenly the sirens went off in Kaya's head. The aunt was probably sixteen and attractive.

"Aha," she said, disappointed, and managed to say, "no big deal."

Even Tracy wondered if he had done his hair for Kaya or if there was a different reason.

Chris continued to look sheepishly at them both. "But you'll take care of it, won't you," he said meekly and gave Sir Whitefoot a treat.

"Of course!" said Kaya and left him standing there.

Tracy's jeep was old and she used it for transporting all sorts of stuff. The back seat was folded down permanently and she always had a lot of straw on top of it, both because she actually transported straw and hay and because that way it was warm and cozy for Chako, her dog. Chako was a cross between a Pharaoh Hound, a German Shepherd and a Husky and, like the stallions, he had plenty of tricks to amaze people with. For instance, he could smile on command, which, with his long shark-like jaw, looked so scary that he made people run for cover.

Today he had stayed home, so the Wild Amazons made themselves comfortable on his bed.

"I'm afraid this isn't exactly legal," said Tracy as she closed the hatchback.

"Rules don't count if you're on your way to do a good deed," said Reni. She sounded so earnest, but the others just snorted with laughter. Kaya got in the front passenger seat.

53

"If you see a uniform and a badge, then just cover yourselves with straw," she said to the girls in the back and got a sneeze as an answer.

"I think I'm allergic to hay," sniffed Cindy. All the girls laughed again.

"A hay allergy! Back at the stable, you always sit with us in the middle of piles of hay," Mia made a crazy sign. "Besides, this stuff is straw."

Cindy responded by sneezing again.

"A straw allergy?" asked Freddy and wrinkled her nose.

"It's probably a dust allergy, since Cindy never has anything like that at her house." They all laughed again because Cindy's mother was famous for being a neat freak.

After she sneezed a third time, Tracy looked at her in the rearview mirror. "Are you sure you want to come along?" Cindy dug in her jeans pocket for a Kleenex and nodded.

"Then here we go!" said Tracy and stepped on the gas.

"And where are we going?" Kaya asked.

"I've got three stables in mind. The people in one of them are pretty odd, sort of a secret society. They don't really know much about anything, but they have good intentions. They would never let a horse deteriorate like that, but they seem to know all the secrets. Maybe they'll have a clue."

"And we're just going to barge in on them?" asked Reni.

"We'll see," Tracy said to the back. "Today is Sunday. They're probably sitting around now. I think they even live in the stalls."

"Not bad," said Mia, "I could picture myself doing that. No more teachers, no more school, just the stable!"

"And then what, your mother will teach you?"

"Home schooling? Hmmm..." said Reni.

"No thanks, I'd rather go to school!" Mia nodded authoritatively.

"As it is, whenever my mother wants to explain something I head for the hills."

"I can't stand that either," admitted Freddy too.

"Although my mother is much better than my father. He has zero patience. If I don't understand something right away, he flips out." Everyone looked at Cindy. She sat leaning against the back window and had the Kleenex pressed to her nose.

"*Your* father flips out?" Reni had to laugh. "Unbelievable!"

Cindy's father was the pastor at the Lutheran church and was known for his endless patience.

"It's just like the shoemaker as father or the dentist

or whatever," explained Cindy and shrugged her shoulders. "Look at Bert; his dad's a dentist and he always has a toothache."

True, somehow their parents' professions never seemed to help the kids very much. On the other hand, thought Kaya, her parents had a restaurant and whenever she was hungry, she always found something delicious to eat. She chose her parents well after all!

Tracy turned onto a wide dirt road that led into the woods. It was sparsely covered with gravel and deep holes.

"What up with this?" asked Freddy. "We must be going to the big bad witch's house from Hansel and Gretel!"

The car jolted from one pothole to the next and the springs groaned and moaned – and the girls complained. "Hey, this is too bumpy!" complained Freddy. "This is worse than on Dagmar!" Dagmar was the Fjord horse in the stable. She could teach anyone who sat on her the true meaning of fear.

"Just go with the flow," said Tracy. "And if we get stuck, then you'll have to get out and push!"

Of course, that was a possibility. The last snowfall, which had already melted off the streets, was still stuck to the ground here in the middle of the woods. The result: a muddy, slippery coating.

"You've got four-wheel drive, so quit making jokes like that!" Kaya was in no mood for another adventure in the cold. Today she wanted things warm and cozy.

The woods opened onto a clearing with paddocks, and in the middle stood a big house and giant barn.

"Wow!" said Kaya, surprised. "I had no idea that there was something like this so close to us..."

"It really does look like a witch's house..." said Freddy.

"Do you think they'll shoot at us?" asked Mia and leaned over to Kaya.

Tracy shook her head. "They're a little odd, but they're peaceful," she said. "They just want to keep to themselves and be left alone."

"But why? Are they survivalists?"

Mia squeezed a little closer to Kaya and Tracy.

"In this cold? Are you nuts?" Kaya shoved her back to the others.

Tracy parked her car behind the barn, next to three similarly decrepit cars.

"Are you a member of their gang, or something?" Reni asked cheekily and made Tracy laugh.

"It sure looks like that, doesn't it," she said, "but this isn't really my thing, although I must admit that it has a certain charm."

The girls gave each other knowing looks and then got out of the car. They marched next to each other, up to the big gate to the courtyard. There was a small door in the big gate and Tracy carefully pushed it open and peeked in.

"Well, what do you see?" asked Kaya. She was extremely impatient and pushed from behind.

Tracy turned around to her and held her pointer finger to her lips. "Shush!" she said.

"Shush?" asked Kaya. "Why shush?"

Tracy repeated the gesture and then slowly went through the door. The five girls followed her in single file. Inside, they had to get used to the dim lighting and the stifling air. Then Kaya saw what Tracy meant when she said the people were odd. The big barn was a cross between a horse pen and a living room. It was all pretty rustic. Cindy's mother would've passed out if she had seen it. There was a big kitchen table in the middle of the room and a few of the adults who sat around it and were playing cards. There were beds against the walls and horses, chickens and dogs in between. One of the dogs had just noticed that six intruders had entered, and he ran up to them, barking and wagging his tail.

Tracy bent down to the indefinable mutt. "Hey, cutie," she said, although the dog was anything but cute. In fact, he was mercilessly ugly, but he immediately nuzzled Tracy and stopped barking.

"Oh Tracy, what an honor!" A man dressed as an old-fashioned farmer got up from the table, shoved a horse that was standing in his way to the side and then walked over to them. He reminded Kaya of a movie she'd seen in the theater. Didn't all the characters in *Braveheart* run around dressed like that? Linen shirt, vest, cloth pants and gaiters. Were they playing medieval times or something?

The man certainly looked the part. His beard was so bushy that you could barely see his eyes, and the big paw he reached out to them – well, it was obvious that they threshed their wheat by hand. The women probably had spinning wheels and looms, too. Kaya secretly pinched her arm. And sure enough, the woman who had stood up was wearing a long wide skirt and a thick woolen shawl around her shoulders. It was hard to tell how old she was. "Welcome to our hall," she said and greeted them with a nod of her head. "Come in!"

The girls looked at each other. What did she mean by "hall" when this was obviously an old barn?

Tracy introduced the girls, while they looked around inquisitively. Sure enough, people and animals, all mixed up together.

"Would you like a glass of water?" asked the woman and caused Cindy to snort.

"Water?" she chirped, but Kaya stomped on her foot. "That's very kind," she said, "but no thank you." The woman nodded. She wore her long, heavy hair open under a light scarf and wore no makeup, but she had an attractive full face. While Tracy was trying to explain why they had come, Kaya noticed six other adults at the table and a whole bunch of children who were staring at them from another corner of the barn. She was dying to know what it was they were up to. What kind of games did children play in the Middle Ages? Wooden wagons with carved horses? Did they always live this way? Or was this just a weekend activity? And if so, how did that work? Listening to Eminem during the week and then listening to their father play lute on the weekend? A thousand questions shot through Kaya's head and she almost missed hearing what the woman was explaining. Two sentence fragments caught her attention: "a cute chestnut pony… yes, a cheeky, playful fellow…"

What were they talking about?

"Well, you heard it yourselves!" said Tracy to the girls.

But Kaya hadn't heard anything… although could she really admit that now? The others nodded. It was

the same as in school when you forgot to pay attention.
If you didn't catch on right away, you were the dummy.
Now she had to ask about what she had missed.

"Okay, then we can get going again," said Tracy and
shook hands with both of them. "Thank you, you've been
a big help," she added. They responded by saying, "God
willing," and then she strode toward the small door.

Outside they all took a deep breath and Cindy had
to sneeze.

"Sure was warm in there," said Freddy, and she
pulled her jacket closed. "Even though they probably
don't even have a heater!"

"On the back wall they have an open fire, which
they cook their food over in the winter," said Tracy,
and she opened the hatchback for the girls. "But the
animals, the hay and the straw – that definitely helps
keep them warm."

Kaya was still dazed. "But that isn't really real," she
said as she got in the car. "I mean, in this day and age,
they can't really live the way people used to a thousand
years ago. They're just doing it for fun, like people play
cowboys and Indians, right?"

Tracy shrugged her shoulders.

"I told you that they're a little different, but
they're very nice. They just happen to prefer a very

different lifestyle. They bake their own bread and draw their water from a well, and who cares, really – lots of people have idiosyncrasies. At least they don't hurt anyone."

Kaya nodded. "And what's up with the horses?"

"Did you space out on everything, Dreamy?" complained Reni. "They sheltered the horses for a while, but the owners didn't look after them, and didn't pay expenses either. They picked them up again after three months. No one knows where the owners brought them after that. That was three months ago."

"October, November, December," Freddy counted out.

"And they didn't know the people?" Kaya asked.

"Sure they did!" Tracyi nodded. "The people gave them their last name, but their phone was disconnected and the address they gave them was phony."

"And they just let them go like that? I would've called the police!"

"You don't really believe that, do you?" Mia wrinkled her forehead. "That they would invite the police into their house of their own free will? An open fire in the stable and who knows what else? They probably chalked it up to bad luck and left it at that."

Tracy started the car.

"Niedermayer. They said the family's name was

Niedermayer. That's not such an everyday name, is it? We should be able to get somewhere with that."

"But what if the name was a fake, too, just like the address?"

Tracy turned the car around behind the barn. A lot of old farm equipment stood around back there: a big hay wagon, a plough, a harrow and a carriage that was covered with a tarp.

"Do you suppose they ride to church in that on Sundays?" Reni said mockingly.

"Don't be a jerk," said Freddy who was just philosophizing out loud about the very different lifestyle they had just seen. "Anyway, that'd be better than hanging around in a barn on Sunday," she said decisively.

"Speaking of church," Tracy said, adjusting the rearview mirror so that she could see Cindy in it, "as a pastor, your father must know all the problem cases in the area. Like the people who have odd hang-ups or are strange in other ways?"

"That's true," Cindy nodded and twirled one of her curls. "And he works with a bunch of different social agencies, so maybe he has an idea. Or maybe there's some sort of register or index or something!"

Tracy nodded and readjusted the rearview mirror

back to where it was. "Okay. Then should we drive you over to your father first or drive to the next farm?"

"To the next farm!" the girls said in unison.

"It looks like you're enjoying yourselves," smiled Tracy.

"This is a lot more fun than TV!" said Mia.

The farm they were driving to next was located closest to the country road where the horses had been found running the night before.

"What kind of a person lives in a place like this?" asked Kaya as they drove up.

"He's the kind of farmer who turns his old cow shed into a horse stable... and instead of milking the cows, he milks the horse owners!"

The girls laughed, but Reni sighed out loud. "Oh golly, I can just imagine the conditions there. I once saw a stable like that in Sayville. The horses live with their own manure all year long, until it's piled as high as the ceiling. Then an excavator comes and hauls everything out and the horses have to jump down nearly two feet onto the cement floor below until the manure piles up all over again. I called the animal protection agency, but they told me it was perfectly normal."

Tracy tried to avoid driving through the potholes and swerved from one side of the road to the other, but

there were just too many potholes. "I think it has less
to do with where you are than who you are," she said.
"Just think about it, stalls are quite an improvement.
Horses used to stand hitched to a post and no one
thought that was odd!"

"But then they probably worked so hard during the
day that they didn't care where they slept at night."
Reni adjusted the straw under her back. "Standing
around in a small box for 23 hours straight isn't very
nice either. Imagine waiting for the one hour of the day
when you can go out, then having to be in top form,
and then having to go back in that grim stall when the
hour is over. That just makes me shake my head!"

"Nothing is perfect," said Kaya and turned around
to the others.

"Except for Chris," trilled Reni. Kaya stuck her
tongue out at her.

The farmer was angry. It was Sunday and he wanted his peace and quiet instead of having to hear about some horse that supposedly ran away.

"No horse breaks out of here if I don't want it to," he said and, looking at his angry, reddened face, the girls took him at his word. No doubt about it, this was one hot-tempered guy with permanently high blood pressure. He was like a pressure cooker. When he slammed his door closed they stood around, unsure of what to do next, although they didn't dare take a look around his stable.

"What would we find there anyway?" Freddy thought out loud. "Even if we saw five empty stalls or hitching posts," she looked over at Tracy, "we still wouldn't know if they ran away from this place."

"They didn't run away. He turned them out!" said Kaya, her voice steady. She looked around. It was one of those typical farms with a main house, a barn and an attached stable. "If these Niedermayers brought their horses here and then didn't bother to show up for months, then I guarantee you that that guy just opened the gates. I'll bet you anything!"

Tracy looked over at the house. "He's watching us," she said quietly. "Let's get into the car and start driving away."

Kaya looked over at the house, too, and sure enough, one of the curtains moved.

"If he's watching us, then it's because he might have something to hide, so my suspicions could be right," she whispered. "Where there's smoke, there's fire."

"Amen!" said Cindy, but nobody laughed.

They drove until they got to the main road, then Tracy pulled onto the shoulder.

"That's less than three miles," she said. "And there's nothing but open fields, not a single fence in the way. I think Kaya is right. We need to think about whether we want to sneak into the stable from the back to look around ourselves."

Kaya felt her heart beat faster.

"He had a big chain leash outside and a doghouse. Probably a real vicious dog, just like his owner," she cautioned the others.

"Maybe there's a way in from the back." Reni bent down between the two front seats. "Most stables have a door in the back, too, not just in the front."

"And inside there'll be a Rottweiler sitting there, excited to have company." Freddy frowned. "Or the old geezer will come out with a shotgun."

"Why don't you just call him up and ask if he has any free stalls, and then we'll know," Cindy suggested.

"That's not a bad idea!" Tracy turned around to her. "We need someone who can fake interest in a stall and then go by and take a look."

"My father!" said Mia right away and they all nodded. Klaus Sonnig was a strong, no-nonsense man and not the sort of person you'd imagine would be faking anything.

"Good idea!" Tracy praised her. "And I'll ask my father if the name Niedermayer means anything to him. Someone who moves around and relocates his horses every three months must have a reason for doing that!" All the girls nodded earnestly.

"Maybe we'll have the case solved by tomorrow!" said Kaya and thought about Sir Whitefoot. If he really was an abandoned pony, then there must be some sort of law about that. Mrs. Walden would know; after all, she was a lawyer. And as long as Kaya needed to talk to her, she could also investigate just how old and decrepit Chris's aunts really were. She started to whistle a happy tune and got a sideways look from Tracy.

"So, are you getting excited about Sir Whitefoot?" she asked sympathetically.

"That too!" said Kaya and couldn't help chortling.

Kaya checked in on Sir Whitefoot and then went over to Dreamy. Both were fine and there was nothing more for her to do. Charlotte would be riding Dreamy this afternoon, which meant Kaya was more or less out of a job.

The big question now was how she should go about approaching Mrs. Walden without it looking too obvious that her main concern was really Chris.

Kaya had a great imagination, but the Waldens lived about six miles away, on the outskirts of the city – you didn't exactly just drop in to say hi if you weren't invited. And she wasn't invited.

Not yet.

Kaya stood at Dreamy's stall and observed her friends going into the clubhouse. Sure, she could do that, too. It was an alternative.

But she was not the kind of person who gave up easily.

It all depended on her getting hold of Mrs. Walden,

and not Chris. She took her cell phone and stood in the farthest corner of the stall so that she was sure that, other than Dreamy, no one could hear her.

She dialed Simone Walden's cell phone number and felt her heart pounding so loudly that she was sure others could hear it, too. Even Dreamy, who was sleeping again with his eyes wide open.

"Walden," she heard and wasn't sure if she could keep her cool.

"Oh Mrs. Walden, I'm sorry if I'm disturbing you in the middle of something. It's Kaya."

"Oh Kaya, no, you're not disturbing me. What's up?"

She was hoping Simone would react to the words "in the middle of something" and talk about the so very important visit from the aunties. But no, nothing.

"We're on the trail of the people who own the five horses!"

"Oh really? How interesting! Tell me about it!"

Kaya briefly talked about the medieval stable and about the nasty old farmer and Simone Walden seemed to find the story quite amusing.

"If Sir Whitefoot really was an abandoned pony, would I legally be allowed to keep him?"

"Let me put it this way: If the owner gave up his

property on purpose, then it is ownerless and that
means you can keep it. It's the same situation if the
owner can't be located – say with a stray cat or an
abandoned dog. But if the animal simply ran away, then
you have to return it to the rightful owner as soon as he
comes forward. If he's looking for it."

"Oh!" Kaya gaped, "then I'll have to stop what I'm
doing immediately! I don't want to have to give him
back!"

She heard Simone laugh. "But even in that case I'm
sure an equitable solution can be found."

That sounded expensive. No, that was silly! She
thought about the lost and found. If the owner didn't
come forward within a certain amount of time, then the
items would be auctioned off. And if no one else joined
in the bidding, then you could snap it up for a bargain
price. A great deal for very little money.

Maybe she could buy Sir Whitefoot for one dollar.
That would be fantastic!

She had to stop Mia and Cindy right away!

"Kaya are you still there?"

Ah yes, she was still on the phone!

"Yes," she stammered, "I was just, well, I have to,
I think I have to think about all this first. By the way,
is Chris there?" That was typical Kaya again. The

thing she absolutely didn't want to ask just slipped right out anyway.

"He's here, but he has company!"

Oh great. Well, now she knew.

"Okay," she said lamely, "no big deal."

"Well, goodbye, Kaya. Don't worry too much about the pony. It'll all work out for the best."

If I only knew what "the best" would be, thought Kaya and hung up.

What a bummer! She was so dumb, so uncool, so hysterical, so totally unprofessional. She really blew it just now. Chris had company and Sir Whitefoot would surely be taken away.

What a lovely turn of events... she could just cry!

Kaya decided to go home. On Sunday afternoon, her family had cake. She would go visit her father in the kitchen and eat a big éclair and maybe a slice of chocolate cake, too, until she felt really nauseated and had a reason to go to bed early. What kind of arguments could she use to hold back Mia and Cindy? There were none. She was being extremely self-centered. That's exactly the way she felt just then, but it wasn't something she could tell anyone else. Not just because it made her look bad, but also because by tomorrow she might change her mind entirely. Her emotions were all over the place, something her mother blamed on puberty, but Kaya knew better. It was the way she was; it was her character.

Kaya had to walk home. That was the downside to her mother driving her to the stable, but the cold air blew some fresh ideas into her head. What was it that Simone Walden had said? It'll all work out for the best.

Well, then she was curious indeed.

The restaurant and the family home formed a single unit and were built connected to each other. That was practical for the parents, because it let them take care of family and business together. But for Kaya and Alexa, it could be pretty annoying sometimes. The worst was when – on their days off – their parents would suddenly remember that they had to take care of a few little things in the restaurant, and then they'd disappear for hours. Kaya went into the kitchen through the back door. Her father was in the middle of stuffing a goose with breadcrumbs, herbs and chopped apple. He was wearing a white apron tied over his jeans and looked surprised as she came in.

"What a rare guest," he said and smiled. She liked her father. He always had a sort of mischievous air about him and seemed younger than her friends' fathers. And he was always in a good mood.

"I hope that isn't Lisa, my favorite goose," she said jokingly as she approached him. She swiped some of the stuffing and popped it in her mouth.

"No, this is Ludwig… but if I know you, I doubt you feel as sorry for the boys."

"Don't be so sure!" Kaya batted her eyelashes coquettishly at him. Then she watched the biathlon. The big birthday present they had given their father last year was a television on a telescopic arm. That way Dad could stay up-to-date and cook at the same time.

"And what brings you home so early?" her father finally asked, but at that moment the door to the restaurant dining room swung open and her mother came in.

"You???" She sounded surprised, too.

"Am I a world wonder or something? You two are acting like I'm almost never here."

"On a Sunday afternoon?" Karin tried to catch her husband's eye. "When who knows what is happening at the stable?"

"Hmm," Kaya said and then she didn't know where she should look.

"Is something up with the new pony?" her mother wanted to know.

"Oh no, he's doing fine!"

"With Dreamy?"

It's appalling when mothers want to be able to share in every conversation.

"No, no, he's okay, too. I was cold and felt like having some cake!"

That was at least partially true.

"Oh," said her mother as she brushed a strand of hair out of her face. "You came at the right time. Alexa just called and wanted to know if she could have some cake, too. If you don't mind, you can take some up to her."

"For Alexa?"

Since when was she her older sister's personal servant?

"And Esther, too. Alexa has a friend over."

That was a good reason. Esther had her driver's license and she knew Chris well. Maybe something would come of this.

Kaya asked for a pot of black tea and then put two slices of cream pie, a slice of cheesecake, and two slices of black forest cherry cake on a cake platter, then put the tea pot, sugar, three cups, three plates, spoons, forks and the cake platter all on a tray and then carried it into the house. As soon as she got to the foyer, she could tell that Esther was there. It smelled like her perfume. Esther always left a trail of perfume that Kaya couldn't stand. She wore way too much and it was way too sweet.

Kaya turned on the light and balanced the big tray as she slowly climbed the stairs to the first floor. Alexa's room was at the top of the stairs on the left side; her own was at the end of the hall on the right. *So, let's see if I can join the ladies*, thought Kaya. She knocked lightly and heard a formal, "Yes, you may enter!" Obviously Alexa thought it was one of the waitresses.

"It's teatime," Kaya trilled as she opened the door. And what she saw was clearly a girls' afternoon: candles, incense, and two glasses of soda were set out on the table between the sofa and the low overstuffed red chair.

They obviously had something they had to discuss. A new love?

She couldn't show any consideration for that now.

"Hey Esther!" she called fervently. "Good to see you. How are you doing?"

Alexa first had to recover from the shock. "What are you doing here, in broad daylight on a Sunday afternoon?"

"There's not all that much daylight left," said Kaya lightly and set the tray down. "It's already four o'clock and it'll be dark soon." She motioned at the cake.

"Mom asked me to bring something up and I figured I'd take along more than enough for all of us." She looked directly at Esther because she could already imagine what kind of expression Alexa had on her face. "Is that okay? Do you like these? There was some apple pie too…"

Esther shook her head. "No, this is just great! Thanks!" She didn't react to Alexa's frown either.

Kaya energetically plunked down on the sofa next to Esther. "It's really nice to be able to relax at home on a Sunday before Christmas!"

She immediately grabbed a plate and asked, "Black forest cherry cake? Cream pie? Or cheese cake?"

Esther turned to her with her cute snub nose, and eyes peering out from under her bangs.

"Well, since you ask, I'd like a big luscious slice of cream pie with lots of whipped cream. I'm totally into that."

"Up until two minutes ago, I thought you were totally into something else," said Alexa archly. Then she reached over, picked up a cup, and held it out to Kaya. "Tea, please!" she said.

Kaya nodded assiduously and served them all tea. Then she grabbed a slice of Black Forest cherry cake and sunk down into the couch.

"So, where did you leave off?" she asked boldly and prepared herself to be thrown out of Alexa's room.

"With boys!" said Alexa venomously. "But that's not a subject you know anything about yet!"

"Oh yeah?" asked Kaya. "Says who?"

Esther had to laugh.

"You're risking a pretty fat lip for a twelve-year-old," warned Alexa.

"Are you trying to insult me?" said Kaya as she stuffed a huge piece of the delicious cake in her mouth. "After all, I'm nearly 14."

"You just turned 13, so don't get carried away."

Older sisters were the most repulsive creatures ever created.

"So? Does that mean that you were a little baby when you were 13 years old?" she provoked her sister. "When you were 13 and I was nine, you acted like you were my mother!"

"And I was, too!" she frowned. "I still am."

Kaya was about to throw the rest of the Black Forest cherry cake at her sister's head, but then Esther made a calming gesture with her hand.

"Come on now," she said. "My half-siblings are still little and believe me, that makes things so much more strenuous. You two can at least have conversations with each other, more or less."

"More or less? More like less!" laughed Alexa.

"You two are just mean!" Suddenly Kaya's eyes were full of tears. Darn, that's exactly what she didn't want to happen. She wanted to stay cool, but she couldn't help herself.

Esther immediately felt remorseful. She put down her plate and put her hand on Kaya's knee. "Hey, I didn't mean it that way."

"I can't help that I'm only 13," sniffled Kaya and rubbed the back of her hand across her eyes.

"I know. Besides, it has its advantages," comforted Esther. "When you're 18, it's really fun at first because suddenly you're allowed to do whatever you want, but then you realize that you have to do a lot of things, too."

"What do you mean?" Kaya sniffed and her gaze fell on Alexa, who was listening attentively. Ah yes, she was still 17. *Ha!* she thought. No need for Alexa to feel so superior.

"Well, suddenly you're responsible for yourself. If you make a mistake, then you have to deal with it alone. If you start going in the wrong direction, then you're the one who has to deal with it a few years down the road or try to set things right again. It makes you think about how nice it used to be when someone would take you in their arms and comfort you!"

"Oh my, listen to us," said Alexa, but she didn't laugh. "Do you suppose it has something to do with the holiday season, that we're suddenly so reflective?"

Kaya ate the rest off her plate. "No idea," she said. "But it seems pretty cool to me to be 18. I mean, you have your driver's license and a car and you can do whatever you feel like doing."

"And if you had a car, what would you do?" Esther wanted to know.

"I'd think of something," said Kaya evasively, because how would she explain to Esther that she'd drive over to Chris's to see if he'd been telling the truth.

They had finished the tea and eaten all of the cake and Alexa's signals were too obvious to be overlooked. She wanted to be rid of her little sister as quickly as possible, but then coincidence came to Kaya's aid. Esther's cell phone rang and boy, did it have a bad ring tone. Kaya tried to be discreet, and turned away from her. She looked around Alexa's room inconspicuously. Alexa had painted it not long ago, and the mixture of orange and red was loud, but it worked. The red chair, the orange-colored bedspread and the long

glass desk with the bright red drawers looked cool.
All the posters of singers or stars that used to hang on
the walls had disappeared. Instead, she had enlarged
and framed photos and placards from plays and
exhibitions. *Maybe I should redecorate my room, too*,
thought Kaya. She did still like her posters, though.
She'd have to rethink that.

Then she heard Esther complain to Alexa, "There
you have it! It's always the same! I constantly have to
babysit the little brats!"

"Me too," rejoined Alexa, but the tone of her voice
and the expression on her face showed that it was a
loving joke. She wanted to make amends for the tears
that fell earlier. Kaya understood that; after all, she
knew her sister well.

"Does that mean you have to go back?" asked Kaya
and tried to disguise the curiosity in her voice. She
smiled, as if she were just making conversation.

"Finn has a show at kindergarten and Laura is out
of control. I have to go keep an eye on Laura so that my
mother can get going with Finn. And, naturally, the father
is unreachable." She gave Kaya a look that spoke volumes.
"That's the advantage of having a driver's license!"

"The other advantage is that you can take me along!"
said Kaya and looked at her lopsidedly.

81

"What do you want in town at this time of day?" asked Alexa immediately, sounding like their mother.

"My school friend Sina lives around the corner from Esther. And it's not even five!"

"Then take care of yourself, little sister, and don't come home too late... the grownups don't like that!" came her sister's reply.

Esther didn't pry. Instead she just let Kaya out at the corner where she'd asked to be dropped off. The new housing development was quite big and Kaya already knew where Esther lived because she wound up there once with Dreamy by accident. She had already liked Chris back then, but she'd been surprised by a thunderstorm and acted uncool. Today she would go about it in a more professional manner. She was already off to a good start: it was dark, she was here and she was going to find out if her feelings for Chris were worth it or not.

Oh gosh, she thought and buried her face in her down jacket, *it is ice cold. Chris is sitting in a warm house and I am totally nuts about him, regardless of how many aunties he has sitting around him.* Still, she was proud of herself. Two hours ago she wouldn't

have believed that she'd manage to do this. But here
she was, proof that you should never underestimate
yourself. She nodded grimly to herself and walked
down the street. The wind blew around her ears, little
snowflakes danced around her and in the glow of the
streetlamp she could see that it had really started to
snow again. She turned around. Her footsteps were
already visible, slightly outward pointing footprints,
all alone on the sidewalk.

Chris's house was set back a bit from the road and
was larger than the neighboring houses. The land was
also flatter and had a larger garden. Although it was also
newly built, there were several trees on the property.
It was very attractive, with a wide driveway and a
generous entrance that was framed by narrow floor to
ceiling windows.

She hadn't thought about that. Kaya stood still.
She had been counting on seeing drawn curtains that
left enough of a crack to sneak a peek, but she hadn't
expected the shutters to be closed! In the first instant
her courage slipped away, but then she got mad.
Shutters should be prohibited – they were simply
inhuman! She looked around and then walked up
the driveway. There was no gate, so she wasn't really
an intruder. Maybe she'd be able to see something

from the back of the house. Simone Walden's jeep stood in the carport. Next to it was a car that she didn't recognize. That was reason to be hopeful. Mr. Walden's BMW was probably parked in the garage. He took special care that it didn't get unnecessarily dirty. Despite the fact that those two were such opposites, thought Kaya, they still seemed to have a happy marriage. Or maybe because of that?

The walkway stones led onto the lawn. The streetlamp didn't shine back here and along the edge of the house it was pretty dark. Kaya tiptoed along carefully, prepared for obstacles, but it was easier that she expected and she got bolder. Behind the house they had built a big, inviting terrace, with steps made of stone that led around its entire perimeter. Flower pots made of terracotta lined the walkway and stood on the terrace. No doubt in the springtime they'd be filled with lush flowers. It certainly was quite grand here.

Kaya got even bolder still. Although the shutters appeared to be closed tight, maybe there was a crack somewhere. She walked up the steps and heard a faint ping and suddenly, everything around her was illuminated.

Oh no! A motion detector!

She quickly looked for a place to hide and ran

behind a bush. But then she noticed her own footsteps in the snow. Any idiot would notice that. One of the shutters clapped open. Her heart beat loudly in her ears and she crouched down and made herself as small as she could. But she couldn't help herself. If she had any chance at all of seeing something, then this was it. And sure enough – Chris came out and next to him was a blonde girl his age.

That was just too much. That jerk! That liar! Kaya wanted nothing more than to jump up, go over to him and punch his arm hard.

Some aunt! As if! What nerve! What a rotten lie!

Stay cool, she told herself. *Kaya, keep your cool, that's your greatest strength*.

"This motion detector is such a pain in the neck!" she heard Chris say.

"Every neighborhood cat sets it off."

She heard someone say something inside, then Chris gracefully stepped back into the house and the shutter was pulled closed once more.

Kaya cowered behind the bush and didn't feel anything any more. Not the cold, not the wind, not even her ice-cold knees. She could have cried right there, but she didn't, she kept her cool.

Kaya needed a good five minutes before she could get out from behind the bush. Now she didn't care if she set off the motion detector or not. She stomped along the side of the house to the front. What a betrayal! She felt queasy and she felt lousy. But on the other hand, he never did give her any real encouragement, did he? But did she want to think about that now? No, she didn't.

She felt terrible, and she had a right to feel terrible. She thought about their first kiss. About how they were standing in the woods on the way to the cabin, and how he kissed her a second time when they were crossing the meadow and how the pony ran away then, but still, the kiss was worth it, so warm, so different – and now it was all supposed to be over?

Her coolness was also over, and she felt the first tears.

And anyway, how was she supposed to get home? She stood on the doorstep of a strange house and the wind blew. It was snowing, her ears hurt and she was the loneliest person in the entire world!

It was all so awful!

Then the light went on again, but this time the houselights illuminated the entrance. Kaya darted behind a car on the other side of the street. She didn't want to miss a thing and watched through the car's windows.

The front door opened and at first nothing happened, but then Simone Walden came out with a woman about the same age who looked a little like her. They took a few steps and then hugged each other and then Simone hugged the man who came out next. And finally, she hugged the blonde girl who waved in the direction of the front door. There stood Chris and his father and in front of them, Charlotte, who had her arms crossed in front of her chest, shivering.

A strange car pulled up and the strange woman and the young blonde girl got in and then the headlights shone exactly in her direction and Kaya ducked and then the car turned onto the street and disappeared. What was that all about? Were they just celebrating an engagement?

Kaya peeked through the car windows again toward the house, but the front door was closed, the light was off and the snowflakes, which were coming down bigger and faster, had covered her tracks.

She straightened up. Well wasn't this great. Now she didn't know any more than she did before. What did all that mean? And whom could she ask?

She looked at the time on her cell phone. It was just after 6 p.m. At 6:30 the bus stopped on the main street, she knew that from Charlotte. When Chris's sister didn't have a ride, she took the bus to the stable.

Every half hour, she said, quite practical. But Kaya didn't have any money on her – that was less practical. And if the bus ran in the evenings, too – well, she had no idea. On top of that, today was Sunday. Still, she started trudging slowly toward the bus stop, and then quickened her step.

The snow came down more heavily and she cursed herself for having had the idea to come out here. Why did she always have to come up with such complicated plans? If only she had stayed with her friends in the clubroom at the stable or at home in her room. She desperately needed to put away her clothes, and her school bag was full of gum wrappers, school announcements to her parents and warnings for not doing her homework three times. She was afraid that she had crunched them all down with her books so badly that she couldn't give any of those papers to anyone any more. Except maybe the invitation to the Christmas party, that was still intact.

But in order to systematically straighten up a school bag, you need to have a certain amount of energy and time, and that was something she didn't have enough of right now. And the mess in her room was also far away. Here she was now, standing at the little bus stop, which was barely noticeable except for a small sign – and there was no covered waiting area. The snow was coming down harder and the only other thing around was the streetlight she was leaning against, as she froze. Her footsteps were already obscured, which was probably not the worst thing to happen, especially in case one of the Waldens happened to go into the garden. But it also gave her a feeling of uncertainty and loneliness. Before long, she'd be completely covered by the snow so that no one could see her. She'd simply not be there any more.

By now it was pitch black out and eerily quiet. She had the feeling that the snow shut out all sounds, that it packed up everything around it in wadding and didn't let anything through to her. She felt the pile of snow on her hair get higher and began to despair that a bus would ever stop here.

Just then she saw the thick wall of snow get a little lighter in the space in front of her. At first she thought it was an illusion, but then she saw there were two lights, and when she heard the motor, it became clear what she was seeing. Unless it was a truck that had lost its way, this could only be the bus.

She dusted the snow off her shoulders and stood closer to the street. The two headlights drilled though the snow and caught her in their glare. Then she heard the squeaky brakes of the red monster. It was the bus. What luck!

The driver looked her over, and then opened the door. She quickly walked up the two steps and immediately felt the warmth inside. She greeted the driver in as friendly a manner as she could muster. The driver, a pleasant middle-aged man nodded at her, shut the door and drove off.

"I didn't expect anyone to actually be waiting at this stop," he said and shook his head.

Kaya didn't know how to react. Should she tell him that she didn't have any money at all with her? She looked around. The bus was empty, which made the situation a little stranger. She was driving through the night in an empty bus.

"I was visiting my friend, but her older brother didn't come to drive me home..." she said and felt her face get red. "And I don't have any money with me at all!" she added quickly.

He looked at her again. She was still standing at the entrance, holding on to the railing.

"It's almost Christmas," he said and smiled. He looked like a big, good-natured teddy bear. "And men are just irresponsible, everyone knows that!" He looked at the road, chewed his gum, and that was that.

"Thanks a lot," said Kaya and sat down on the front seat. The red fabric was warm and the security of the bus made her sleepy. She could have ridden like this forever.

"Where do you need to go?" asked the bus driver after a little while. They had just passed the city limits of their small town.

"Anywhere along this main street is fine. I have to go to the 'Landsknecht' restaurant, if you know where that is."

"Oh, are you from there?" He looked interested.

"My parents own it!" said Kaya, feeling a little shy and a little proud at the same time.

"I stop in there for a drink every so often," he said and nodded. "Good place!"

They drove along the main road, and when the driver turned off and drove the big red bus right up to her parents' restaurant, Kaya couldn't believe her eyes.

"You probably aren't really a bus driver at all – but a guardian angel instead," she said and shook his hand before getting off.

"Like I said, it's almost Christmas," his eyes twinkled.

"Thank you so much!" Kaya jumped out and watched the taillights drive away until they disappeared. Amazing!

She quickly went into the restaurant and to her father in the kitchen to see if there was anything she could snack on.

"Did I just see a bus?" he asked her incredulously,

although he was so busy deglazing a roast that he quickly forgot his own question.

He arranged Brussels sprouts, wide noodles and a slice of the roast on a plate for Kaya and drizzled it with some of the aromatic brown gravy. She quickly thanked him and sat down at the small table that stood under the television. She loved her father's kitchen, the hustle, and the ingredients that came and what he made with them. Besides, it was warm here, and it was so endlessly cozy to sit here and watch him cooking. She used to do that a lot, although lately not at all. She thought about why that might be. She figured it was because she didn't have enough time anymore. Or had her preferences somehow changed?

Her cell phone rang.

She looked quickly at her father. He found it annoying when she was constantly on the phone. But she hadn't made a single phone call all day – well, almost none.

It was Cindy.

"Can you come down to the stable right away?" Kaya looked at her watch. It was almost eight.

"Hmm!" she grunted. The next day was a school day, so she had to come up with a really important reason. "Why?"

"My father knew right away who it was. We want to go there right away!"

The fork dropped out of Kaya's hand. Oh my gosh! Was that good news or bad news? What could it mean for her, and for Sir Whitefoot?

She swallowed. Right at that moment, her mother came in with a tray full of dirty dishes. She set it down next to the sink, grabbed a new tray, put a few plates of food that were ready to go on it and was ready to go back out again when she noticed Kaya.

She stopped for a minute.

"Nice to see you," she said and smiled at her. "Is everything okay?"

"Everything's great, Mom!"

"I'm afraid we're going to have a late night tonight. We've got a bunch of Christmas parties. Can I rely on you?"

"Sure, Mom!"

Her mother kissed in her direction and rushed through the swinging door back into the dining room.

So, she was good to go. No one would check her room before midnight.

She put her empty plate in the sink, gave her father a kiss on the cheek; in return he gave her a little pinch and then she was on her way out the door. "Everything okay?" her father still wanted to know.

"Everything's okay!" she answered.

Less than half an hour later she was at the stable. She had turned on a light, turned on her radio, grabbed some warmer clothes out of the pile in front of her closet, pulled on warm boots that she would never wear outside during the day because they looked so nerdy, and then got going. She felt pretty bad about sneaking out, but she just didn't feel like having a discussion and really, her parents obviously didn't have time right then to talk. So all she had done was shorten the whole process.

Her friends were sitting in the clubroom, along with Cindy's father and Claudia. Kaya had expected a bigger group, but maybe it was better if they didn't make too big a deal out of it. She nodded to all of them and then sat down next to Mia. She would have loved to burst out with all her questions, but she didn't want to interrupt. Cindy's father was speaking and everyone was listening with rapt attention. Then the door opened and Simone Walden came in with Chris. Kaya didn't know where to look. Could she ever look at those two unself-consciously again?

"You gave us a call?" said Simone to Claudia, and

the riding teacher nodded and motioned them to the bench. Kaya moved over to make room for Simone and Chris. So now this traitor was sitting next to her, too. She nodded coolly to him and made a show of leaning forward to listen to Cindy's father. He had stopped talking to wait for the group to quiet down again.

"We would have gotten here earlier," said Simone, "but my sister was visiting and we couldn't get away any faster."

So, her sister. With her daughter. The cute blonde cousin who was probably fun to flirt with. Kaya felt her temperature rise.

She stood around in the cold for hours for this! It was downright mean!

Claudia waved her comments aside and nodded to Cindy's father, Mr. Logan.

The Lutheran pastor, casual in a flannel shirt, nodded back at her as he collected himself again.

"Okay," he said, "I'll explain again briefly. When Cindy told me about the five horses, I had an idea, but I wasn't sure. I don't believe it would have made any sense checking out that farmer's stable, though, and whether or not he had any empty stalls there. Besides, he definitely wouldn't admit of his own free will that he had put five animals in a life-threatening situation – for the animals and for other people. I know the man. He can be extremely cranky."

He took a sip of his tea.

"But I do know that there's a family with three children that fell on some very hard times. The husband had a good job and the wife worked part-time so that she'd have enough time for the children, who are eight, ten and thirteen years old."

Kaya and Mia looked at each other. That was how old they were.

"They had built a house, had horses and a dog and life looked rosy."

Mr. Logan took a deep breath and it was so quiet you could hear a pin drop.

"But then the wife got sick and the husband couldn't manage caring for her and the children and got behind in his job. Before long, he was fired and couldn't find a new job. And all the while the costs for the house were eating up all their savings. They had to sell it, but got far less for it than it was worth. Then they moved to an apartment and couldn't afford that either and then wound up as a welfare case."

No one said a word. "They didn't want to give up the horses, so they took them by foot from one stable to the next and got kicked out every time they couldn't pay upkeep. They didn't have any money for the veterinarian or the farrier, and in the end the whole thing collapsed." His gaze swept the room and stopped at Kaya. "Last night."

Kaya nodded. That was just awful. She thought about her own parents. What would happen if her mother or her father got sick?

"That's where things stand now," he said finally and reached for his mug.

Simone Walden interrupted the silence. "And what can we do?" she asked simply. "Should we go to these people?"

Mr. Logan slowly shook his head.

"It's especially rough on the children. They don't want to out themselves as being poor or their friends would drop them."

"Not with us!" protested Kaya and the others quickly nodded.

The pastor frowned slightly, which made him look like a seal. "Come on, be honest: if someone is hanging out with you who doesn't wear the same clothes as you, doesn't have money for the newest CDs, is never able to go along when you plan something – how long is someone like that still interesting to you?"

They looked at each other and each went through a mental list of everyone else at school.

That was true enough that you didn't want to have anything to do with some people, but did that have anything to do with brand names? There were just some people you didn't like. They bragged, or were deceitful, snotty or just boring. Kaya didn't think that it had anything to do with superficial things like brand name clothing, but that wasn't something that mattered to her anyway. On the other hand, if one of the children was 13 years old, then someone had to know that person. There weren't all that many schools in this area.

"And why shouldn't we go there?" said Kaya, taking up Simone's suggestion.

"I understand," said Mrs. Walden. "How would we feel if we didn't have anything left of the stuff that meant so much to us today, and were sitting around in an apartment that we don't like and then a bunch of people barge in, looking at us as if we were at the zoo, asking all kinds of dumb questions."

"That's not the way it would be!" said Cindy. "We wouldn't just stare. Besides, maybe we could help somehow!"

"First off, we're helping the horses, and that already helps these people."

"But in the past few weeks they haven't done anything themselves for the animals!" Freddy wasn't convinced yet. "They didn't even check in on their horses anymore. That's what those medieval types told us!"

Claudia looked at her, but Freddy gave her a dismissive wave. "It doesn't matter anyway."

"If the story is true, then they couldn't just show up there again. They would have expected money or would have made the family take their horses back. Neither of those was an option for them." Chris got in on the discussion but Kaya gave him a look. If he weren't so incredibly good-looking, then she wouldn't care one bit about any old cousin. Not one single bit!

"Of course the story is true... or are you trying to tell us that a Lutheran pastor tells lies?" Kaya snapped at Chris so that he looked at her, totally surprised.

"No, of course not," he said, and looked at Mr. Logan.

"So there!" Kaya added.

"All right already," Simone Walden tried not to smile. "But let me ask the question again: What can we do?"

Claudia took a deep breath. "Does the family have any chance of getting back on their feet?"

Cindy's father took a deep breath. He thought about it. Then he slowly shook his head. "Not in the near future." He wiped his brow. "The wife had cancer, was operated on and, sad to say, it's still not clear if she'll recover."

"Oh no," said Simone. "Then the children might even lose their mother?"

It was quiet again and Kaya felt the tears well up in her eyes. To lose your own mother was a horrible thought.

"No one said that would happen," said Mr. Logan gently, trying to soften the statement. "She could get better."

They looked at each other. This case was much worse than they had originally thought.

"Then we'll have to sell the horses," said Claudia. There's nothing else we can do. We'll look for good homes for the animals, but the situation as it is now doesn't benefit anyone. Not the animals and not the family either. By selling them, at least the family will have some money."

Chris nodded. "Why haven't they done that themselves?"

"Why," Kaya imitated him. "Because they're attached to their horses."

"What is up with you?" asked Chris, wrinkling his forehead.

"Nothing," said Kaya and tried to smile, although it looked more like a grimace.

"Do you think they'll take it as good news if they hear that we're trying to find a good home for their horses?" Simone Walden leaned forward. So did Claudia.

"I think so," said Mr. Logan. "They'll be happy that someone who understands the business is taking care of it for them."

Claudia and Simone nodded to each other. "We'll take care of it," said Claudia. "And we should include Tracy in this, too – she really knows her stuff!"

Simone agreed and Kaya leaned back. What did this mean for Sir Whitefoot? If someone could pay more for him than she could, then he'd be gone. This was just like what happened with Flying Dream. Once again she didn't have a chance.

Mr. Logan was right: without money, life could be terribly difficult.

The week dragged. Wednesday morning Kaya told
her parents everything that had happened on Sunday,
about the search for the horses' owners with Tracy, and
she confessed to going to the meeting in the stable that
evening. She left out her little outing to the Walden
house. The worst that could happen was that the bus
driver might have one too many drinks at her parents'
restaurant and spill the beans to her mother one day.

There were holiday celebrations at school and, as a
friendly gesture, the school sent roses to other schools.
No one took classes very seriously at the moment.
After all, it was almost the holidays, so how were they
supposed to think about math, anyway? Some of the
kids were already dreaming about their upcoming
skiing vacations, and others were trying to figure out
if the presents they were hoping for would really turn

up under the Christmas tree. Kaya thought about the holiday pageant and trained alternately with Dreamy and Wild Thing. Ever since she'd heard the story of how the family had lost everything, she realized that she was very lucky. She didn't have a horse of her own, but she had every opportunity to ride terrific horses and didn't even have to pay anything. That gave her an idea, and one afternoon she phoned Mr. Logan. His first reaction was to call his daughter to the phone, but Kaya told him she wanted to talk to him and not Cindy.

Kaya told him she thought that the children should get an opportunity to ride the horses.

"If they can ride well," she said, "then that's something that should be communicated. A lot of people are happy when their horses are cared for and exercised, and you know everyone around here, I mean, more people, more riders and more stables than we do!" He heard her out and then he promised to think about her idea. It wasn't a bad one at all.

People were already streaming into the hall an hour before the Christmas pageant was scheduled to start. It was huge and the enormous crowd made Kaya afraid. The audience had never been this big. Would there be enough seating on the hay bales? But the mood was excellent. People streamed past the stalls and the horses despite all the signs that strictly prohibited that, armed against the cold with mulled cider and hot dogs. People were exhilarated and shared the latest gossip. Kaya struggled to get her ponies ready. As usual, everything came together in the last second, and when the host greeted the audience and got them in the mood for two hours' worth of entertainment, all the performers were standing in the wings, waiting to go on.

First Kai and Romke, the two beautiful Friesians, entered the arena pulling the red-ribboned carriage in which the chairman and guests of honor were riding. They made three turns around the arena, which looked festive with colorful decorations. After the opening ceremony, the pageant was ready to start.

The youth quadrille rode in first. They had practiced the most and, as a result, they had the lowest chance of having something go wrong. Kaya rode on Wild Thing next to Mia on her Haflinger Luxury Illusion, and together they formed the front. Behind them rode their friends and other girls, including Charlotte, who was riding her pony, Flying Dream. During training Kaya always kept an eye on her, but today she had to concentrate fully on Wild Thing.

Rick, Claudia's husband, had strewn white sawdust

in the middle of the arena so that it formed a big, bright star. In addition, the entire hall was decorated with pine branches and red ribbons, and hundreds of small candles in thick glass holders had been placed all along the ring fence. It was a truly thrilling scene, but for the horses it was something else: completely unusual and, as such, frightening. The first thing Luxury wanted to do was to jump to the side as Mia guided him through the masses of people sitting on the hay bales. Mia was able to work against that impulse and guide him back onto the lane leading into the arena. But the whole scene still made the white horse uneasy.

While Wild Thing was totally relaxed about performing her exercises, Luxury tensed at every corner, which told Mia that she was sitting on a powder keg. Still, their performance went well. They received an enthusiastic round of applause, which caused the Haflinger to bolt. Somehow they all managed to get out of the ring in one piece as they made room for the next act.

It had been announced as a "Pas de deux," although it wasn't quite what the knowledgeable members of the audience expected, namely an elegant dressage presentation by two horses. Instead, the doors swung open and in came Nike, a cute white horse ridden by

Mia, who had quickly changed mounts outside the arena, followed by Vinchita. A murmur went through the audience and that was exactly what Claudia was hoping for. Vinchita was Nike's foal, a light gray ball of fleece with a white blaze that bounded through the arena while Mia rode a normal dressage with Nike. Anyone who saw her wanted to take that fluffy little foal home to cuddle. She was a dream, and not just for the children.

When Mia stopped at the middle line to greet the audience, Vinchita ran over to them in front of the entire audience and – despite the unusual atmosphere – she collected her reward in the form of milk from her mother. She took her time suckling. People were so moved that tears started to well up in their eyes, and when the door swung out for the two horses, the audience applauded them excitedly.

It couldn't have been more of a contrast to what came next: Brioso, the coal black Andalusian rode in at Tracy's side. Tracy was slim and slender while the stallion was a pack of muscles. Tracy wore a white ruffled blouse with a long Spanish riding skirt. Brioso had nothing more than a black snaffle. She held him on a thin leather cord, and when they reached the middle of the arena loud Spanish guitar music came on and

Brioso did a curtsy for the audience, bowing deeply and then proudly getting up again. Brioso was such a vision of strength and grace coupled with extraordinary charisma that everyone watched him with bated breath.

Brioso, whose name, the announcer explained, meant "fiery one," crossed the arena with a Spanish walk, lay down on command and stood up again. But when he stood up on his hind legs and approached Tracy as she backed away step by step, the audience held its collective breath. Standing up like that, he seemed to be three times as big as Tracy. Everyone would have loved to photograph him that way, but taking photographs was not allowed. After this impressive performance, it was time for the adult quadrille. Claudia's idea was that Brioso's strong impression would take away from any mistakes the next group made, but her precaution turned out to be unnecessary. Amazingly enough there were only a few small missteps that no one noticed because everything else came off without a hitch.

"I'll never hold another dress rehearsal," Claudia whispered to her husband. The announcer heard her remark and included it in his commentary. Vaulting on Kai was up next. The little ones were doing great and the black horse completed it with a sense of calm as if he had never done anything else in his life. The Friesian gave a protective air as he evenly and carefully galloped through his rounds on the lunge and allowed the little girls and boys to play on his back.

And then came the jumping quadrille. While fresh mulled cider was being served, volunteers quickly set up the obstacles in the middle of the track and the girls mounted their ponies. They had adorned their horse – and themselves – with silver stars. Dreamy fidgeted under Kaya. He heard the music and wanted to get going. But they were still standing in front of the closed door sto the arena and had to wait. They concentrated on what they needed to do next and Kaya was going over the individual positions in her head when she felt a hand on her boot. Chris stood next to her. She was startled, but pleased, too.

"Have I told you that my cousin is pretty, and dumb as a turkey?"

Kaya had to take a deep breath.

"Are you sure?" she asked.

"Of course. I always have to be there when my aunt brings her, and then she babbles on and on about things that don't interest me at all!"

"Really?"

"Yes! And she doesn't understand the first thing about riding!"

109

That was the clincher. A wide grin spread over Kaya's face. "She doesn't understand a thing?"

"Like I said, she's dumb!"

His hand was still on her boot and his brow was furrowed. He looked so cute and his gaze up at her was simply divine.

"Okay then," said Kaya and rewarded him with a smile.

"Hah!" she called, but that wasn't aimed at Chris. Just then the gate opened and the four ponies galloped full speed ahead onto the track. The light in the arena reflected off the stars they had stuck on, giving it an extra special charm while the young Amazons swept through the obstacles, riding ever wilder and faster. The audience held its collective breath once again for some of the jumps because it looked as if the Amazons were sure to crash into each other.

But it all came off without the slightest hitch, and when the music stopped and the girls stood still in the middle of the arena in the formation of a star, the audience went wild. They truly rode like warriors, and next they were applauded individually as the announcer introduced each of the girls with her pony. Kaya on Flying Dream, Mia on Luxury Illusion, Frederica – nicknamed Freddy – on Snoopy and Reni on Don Juan.

They got another loud round of applause, and because
Claudia had anticipated that, the girls had prepared an
encore. They swept through the arena one more time,
shooting from left to right and right to left over the
obstacles, and when the gates out of the arena opened
for them they could hear the announcer say, "Yes, Ladies
and Gentlemen, those girls are our 'Wild Amazons'!"

"Cool!" said Kaya as she slid off Dreamy and felt
completely happy. If only you could save up the good
feelings for bad days, she thought, like chocolate or
potato chips, then she could always have a portion
when her mood was sour.

But she didn't have much time for such philosophical
musings. One of the helpers took Dreamy from her
because now it was time for the evening's highlight. The
four rescued horses and the pony stood there, groomed
and polished. Their hooves were trimmed and dressed,
their manes were braided, their tails were washed
and brushed, and silver bows decorated their hair and
snaffles. Each of the girls took one and together they
walked into the arena in single file. Claudia had taken the
microphone and was retelling the story of the dramatic
night, the rescue effort and their lodging in the stable,
a story that certainly fit in with the Christmas story of
Mary, Joseph and baby Jesus in the manger.

Everyone was absolutely silent, so that you could have heard a pin drop. Even the horses stood as still as statues. "Now it's up to us to give these animals a new, and good home, and to help their owners who have suffered such great misfortune through no fault of their own."

She waited a moment, but nobody said a word. "If anyone out there is looking for a recreational horse, a friend to explore the world with and ride across fields and through forests, then please listen closely. Tonight is your opportunity to do a good deed – for people and animals."

It was still totally silent.

Suddenly a hand went up and Claudia passed the microphone into the dark audience. A voice spoke loudly and clearly: "My wife and I would like to give our daughter Kaya the pony that she helped rescue, her Sir Whitefoot. We love her and now she can share this love!"

"Daddy!" Kaya screamed loudly and embraced Sir Whitefoot's neck because she couldn't get to her father as quickly.

And the pony snorted, as if it fully understood that this was the HAPPY ENDING.